Fins On

Just Right Reader

"Look, a map!"

"Liz, pin the map up."

"Dad, it has an X."

"Zip it up, Liz."

"Fins on, Dad!"

"Sit. You go in."

"Dig it up, Dad!"

"Hit it, Liz."

A big win!

We did it!

Phonics Fun

- Write the words from the list on a piece of paper.
- With a partner, take turns reading the words.

dig fin hit pin

High Frequency Words

go   we   you

Comprehension

Who was the main character in the story?

Decodable Words

big	Liz
did	pin
dig	sit
fin	win
hit	zip

15